The Truth About
Hansel
and Gretel

By Karina Law

Illustrated by Elke Counsell

Special thanks to our advisers for their expertise:

Adria F. Klein, Ph.D.
Professor Emeritus, California State University
San Bernardino, California

Susan Kesselring, M.A.
Literacy Educator
Rosemount-Apple Valley-Eagan (Minnesota) School District

PiCTURE WiNDOW BOOKS
Minneapolis, Minnesota

Levels for *Read-it!* Readers

- Familiar topics
- Frequently used words
- Repeating patterns

- New ideas
- Larger vocabulary
- Variety of language structures

- Challenges in ideas
- Expanded vocabulary
- Wide variety of sentences

- More complex ideas
- Extended vocabulary range
- Expanded language structures

A Note to Parents and Caregivers:

Read-it! Readers are for children who are just starting on the amazing road to reading. These beautiful books support both the acquisition of reading skills and the love of books.

The RED LEVEL presents familiar topics using common words and repeating sentence patterns.

The BLUE LEVEL presents new ideas using a larger vocabulary and varied sentence structure.

The YELLOW LEVEL presents more challenging ideas, a broad vocabulary, and wide variety in sentence structure.

The GREEN LEVEL presents more complex ideas, an extended vocabulary range, and expanded language structures.

When sharing a book with your child, read in short stretches, pausing often to talk about the pictures. Have your child turn the pages and point to the pictures and familiar words. And be sure to reread favorite stories or parts of stories.

There is no right or wrong way to share books with children. Find time to read with your child, and pass on the legacy of literacy.

Adria F. Klein, Ph.D.
Professor Emeritus
California State University
San Bernardino, California

First American edition published in 2005 by
Picture Window Books
5115 Excelsior Boulevard
Suite 232
Minneapolis, MN 55416
877-845-8392
www.picturewindowbooks.com

First published in Great Britain by Franklin Watts, 96 Leonard Street,
London, EC2A 4XD

Printed in the United States of America.

Library of Congress Cataloging-in-Publication Data
Law, Karina.
The truth about Hansel and Gretel / by Karina Law ; illustrated by Elke Counsell.
p. cm. — (Read-it! readers)
Summary: The owner of the gingerbread house that Hansel and Gretel came upon in the
woods tells her side of the story.
ISBN 1-4048-0559-1 (hardcover)
[1. Fairy tales. 2. Humorous stories.] I. Counsell, Elke, ill. II. Hansel and Gretel. English.
III. Title. IV. Series.
PZ8.L4345Tr 2004
398.2—dc22   2004007334

This is my house. Isn't it beautiful?
The walls are made of gingerbread,
and the roof is made of toffee.

I decorated it myself with all my
favorite sweets.

I suppose you have read the stories about me. They are all false, you know. I'm not really a witch. I'm just a harmless old lady.

Once upon a time, I was very happy, living in my beautiful house in the woods.

Then those terrible children came along and spoiled everything.

I spotted them from my window.

Hansel and Gretel were their names.

I don't get many visitors, so I was
going to invite them in for a nice
cup of tea.

Imagine how angry I was when I
opened the door to find them
eating my beautiful house!

My new sugar windows had just been put in, and that naughty boy was snapping off part of a peppermint window frame.

13

His nasty sister was licking one of
the strawberry lollipops on my
wall. What a pest!

I shouted at them to stop, and do you know what those rude children did?

They yelled, "Leave us alone, you old witch!"

As you can imagine, I was really angry, and I started scolding those naughty children.

But they just laughed and ran
straight past me into my house!

You won't believe what happened next. I followed the children into the house, and, just as I was asking where they lived, that awful boy pushed me into the oven.

His horrid sister was no better. The terrible pair ran away, laughing.

I was left with my head stuck in a
pot of stew!

Then, to make matters worse,
those awful children told terrible
lies about me. The shame of it!

Hansel told people that I locked

him up. What a story!

And Gretel said that I was a witch who liked scaring children. What a wicked thing to say!

Life has never been the same since the stories about me were printed in the local newspaper.

I don't get any visitors now.

People are afraid of me.

After all the horrible stories
Hansel and Gretel told, people
think I'm a witch.

But you can see I'm not. Can't you?

Levels for *Read-it!* Readers

Read-it! Readers help children practice early reading skills with brightly illustrated stories.

Red Level: Familiar topics with frequently used words and repeating patterns.

I Am in Charge of Me by Dana Meachen Rau
Let's Share by Dana Meachen Rau

Blue Level: New ideas with a larger vocabulary and a variety of language structures.

At the Beach by Patricia M. Stockland
The Playground Snake by Brian Moses

Yellow Level: Challenging ideas with an expanded vocabulary and a wide variety of sentences.

Flynn Flies High by Hilary Robinson
Marvin, the Blue Pig by Karen Wallace
Moo! by Penny Dolan
Pippin's Big Jump by Hilary Robinson
The Queen's Dragon by Anne Cassidy
Sounds Like Fun by Dana Meachen Rau
Tired of Waiting by Dana Meachen Rau
Whose Birthday Is It? by Sherryl Clark

Green Level: More complex ideas with an extended vocabulary range and expanded language structures.

Clever Cat by Karen Wallace
Flora McQuack by Penny Dolan
Izzie's Idea by Jillian Powell
Naughty Nancy by Anne Cassidy
The Princess and the Frog by Margaret Nash
The Roly-Poly Rice Ball by Penny Dolan
Run! by Sue Ferraby
Sausages! by Anne Adeney
Stickers, Shells, and Snow Globes by Dana Meachen Rau
The Truth About Hansel and Gretel by Karina Law
Willie the Whale by Joy Oades

A complete list of *Read-it!* Readers is available on our Web site:
www.picturewindowbooks.com